Joseph
AND THE
Sabbath Fish

This
PJ BOOK
belongs to

_____

_____

KAR-BEN PUBLISHING, INC.
A division of Lerner Publishing Group
241 First Avenue North
Minneapolis, MN 55401 U.S.A.
1-800-4-Karben

Website address: www.karben.com

Library of Congress Cataloging-in-Publication Data

Kimmel, Eric A.
    Joseph and the Sabbath fish / by Eric A. Kimmel ; illustrated by Martina Peluso.
      p.   cm.
    Summary: Retells the story of Joseph, who is rewarded for honoring the Sabbath by being
generous to others even after he, himself, becomes poor.
    ISBN 978-0-7613-5908-1 (lib. bdg. : alk. paper) [1. Folklore. 2. Sabbath--Folklore. 3.
Jews--Folklore.]
      I. Peluso, Martina, ill. II. Title.
  PZ8.1.K567Jos 2011

398.2'36089924--dc2   2009043791

PJ Library Edition ISBN 978-0-7613-7955-3

Manufactured in Hong Kong
2-45249-12300-12/19/2017

061826K2/B1241/A5

Joseph
AND THE
Sabbath Fish

Eric A. Kimmel

illustrated by Martina Peluso

KAR-BEN
PUBLISHING

Long ago, a man named Joseph lived in the land of Israel. He made his home in Tiberias, a city on the shores of the Sea of Galilee.

No one honored the Sabbath more than Joseph. No one set a more elegant table. His challah loaves were baked with the finest flour. His goblets were filled with the rarest wine. The fish for his Sabbath meal was the sweetest that could be found. Perfumed oil pressed from the ripest olives filled his Sabbath lamps.

Every Friday night as the sun began to set, Joseph threw open the doors of his house. He invited anyone who wished to celebrate the Sabbath to come in.

Travelers far from home, beggars from the alleys, young and old, rich or poor, everyone was welcome. Joseph treated them all as honored guests.

Joseph's neighbor Judah also set a fine Sabbath table. But he did not open his house to everyone.

"Why do you waste money feeding beggars?" Judah asked Joseph. "They would be satisfied with less. Do as I do. Give charity to the beggars, but invite only important people to your Sabbath table."

"Everyone is important," said Joseph. "Those who come to my table are honoring me, and together we honor the Sabbath. What we give to the Sabbath is repaid a thousandfold."

"Wait and see. You will be left with nothing," Judah predicted.

Over time, Judah's warning came true. Joseph's wealth melted away. He no longer lived in a fine house. He no longer dressed in expensive clothes. But he still celebrated the Sabbath, and he still welcomed everyone to his home. Now his guests baked the challah, brought the fish, and shared their wine. His lamps were filled with ordinary oil, but the joy around his table was the same.

Judah scoffed as he saw Joseph's fortunes decline. "What we give to the Sabbath is repaid a thousandfold? What a joke! Joseph's hospitality has brought him to the gutter."

Then one night Judah had a dream. He saw Joseph sitting in his house, overseeing his lands, and counting his money as if it were his own. Judah woke up trembling.

"Does this mean that all my wealth will be given to Joseph?" he worried. "Is this dream a warning?"

Judah became so frightened that he could not sleep. He avoided Joseph, and if he saw him by chance, he ran away. His terror became so great that he sold everything he owned and purchased a ruby as big as a hazelnut. He sewed the ruby into the lining of his felt cap. Then he packed his clothes and left Tiberias.

Judah traveled to the port city of Caesarea, where he boarded a ship bound for Africa. "Joseph will never find me," he thought to himself. "I will be safe at last."

After several days at sea, the ship sailed into a frightful storm. The sailors and passengers clung to the rigging to keep from being swept overboard. A gust of wind whipped Judah's cap from his head and tossed his life's savings into the churning waves.

Back in Tiberias, Joseph still celebrated the Sabbath, even though his fortunes continued to decline. He missed his friend Judah and wondered why he had left so suddenly.

One day he went down to the market to shop for the Sabbath. A fisherman had just brought a huge, fat fish to the dock.

"Look at that one!" Joseph exclaimed. "What a Sabbath meal that fish would make!"

"Take it!" the fisherman said.

"I can't do that. You have to earn a living, too," said Joseph.

"Don't you remember me, Joseph?" the fisherman asked. "Last year I lost my boat in a storm. You welcomed my family to your home and shared your Sabbath meal with us. You invited us to come back every Sabbath, and you helped me find a new boat. I owe everything to you. Allow me to repay some of my debt. Please take the fish."

"On one condition," Joseph said. "You and your family must come to my house this Sabbath to help me eat it."

Joseph took the fish home. When his wife cut it open, she saw something glistening. When she looked closer, she discovered a ruby as large as a hazelnut.

"We're rich!" she cried.

"What a fine Sabbath we will have!" Joseph exclaimed.

Joseph sold the ruby for thirteen sacks of gold. He bought back his house and lands. He prospered as never before, but his greatest joy was still in celebrating the Sabbath.

One Friday evening a weary traveler appeared at Joseph's door. "Come celebrate the Sabbath with us," Joseph said, inviting him in.

"Don't you recognize me, Joseph?" the traveler said. "I am your friend Judah. I was once rich, but now I have lost everything." He described how he had become penniless when his ruby was lost in a storm.

Joseph embraced Judah. "I am so happy to see you. I found your ruby, and I will return its value to you."

"No," Judah replied. "In my long travels I have learned that some things are more important than riches. Your friendship is one. And the peace and joy of the Sabbath day is most precious of all."

With Joseph's help, Judah regained his wealth. And from then on he celebrated the Sabbath as Joseph did, with an open door and an open heart.

For truly it is said, what we give to the Sabbath is repaid a thousandfold.

ABOUT THE AUTHOR AND ILLUSTRATOR

Eric A. Kimmel has been writing for children for over 40 years. His more than 100 titles include such classics as *Anansi and the Moss-Covered Rock*, *Hershel and the Hanukkah Goblins*, and *The Chanukkah Guest*. A native New Yorker, he now lives in Portland, Oregon. His hobbies include playing bluegrass banjo, riding horses and bicycles, and caring for his tropical fish, two cats, and pet snake.

Martina Peluso studied at the Art Institute of Naples. She has illustrated several children's books, and her art has been exhibited throughout the world. She lives in Naples, Italy, where she shares a house with her cats, Peppe and Ernesto.